SHELLY

MARGIE PALATINI

Illustrated by GUY FRANCIS

✳ Dutton Children's Books ✳

✳ *Dutton Children's Books* ✳

A DIVISION OF PENGUIN YOUNG READERS GROUP

Published by the Penguin Group

Penguin Group (USA) Inc., 375 Hudson Street, New York, New York 10014, U.S.A. ✳

Penguin Group (Canada), 90 Eglinton Avenue East, Suite 700, Toronto, Ontario, Canada

M4P 2Y3 (a division of Pearson Penguin Canada Inc.) ✳ Penguin Books Ltd, 80 Strand,

London WC2R 0RL, England ✳ Penguin Ireland, 25 St Stephen's Green, Dublin 2, Ireland

(a division of Penguin Books Ltd) ✳ Penguin Group (Australia), 250 Camberwell Road,

Camberwell, Victoria 3124, Australia (a division of Pearson Australia Group Pty Ltd) ✳

Penguin Books India Pvt Ltd, 11 Community Centre, Panchsheel Park, New Delhi - 110 017,

India ✳ Penguin Group (NZ), Cnr Airborne and Rosedale Roads, Albany, Auckland 1310,

New Zealand (a division of Pearson New Zealand Ltd) ✳ Penguin Books (South Africa)

(Pty) Ltd, 24 Sturdee Avenue, Rosebank, Johannesburg 2196, South Africa ✳ Penguin

Books Ltd, Registered Offices: 80 Strand, London WC2R 0RL, England

CIP Data is available.

Published in the United States by Dutton Children's Books,

a division of Penguin Young Readers Group

345 Hudson Street, New York, New York 10014

www.penguin.com/youngreaders

Designed by Heather Wood

Manufactured in China

First Edition

ISBN 0-525-47565-6

1 3 5 7 9 10 8 6 4 2

For Raymond and Barbara
—M.P.

To Janet
—G.F.

Shelly was not ready.

Not ready like his sister Adelaide.
"Nope."

Not ready like his sister Miranda.
"Uh-uh."

Not at all ready according to
his sister Tallulah.
"Definitely not."

Not that it mattered to Shelly.
Not that it mattered one bit.

But it mattered very much to his sisters.
They could be most impatient.

"He's fine," said Father. "Wait and see."
So they waited.
"We don't see a thing," said the three.
"He's taking his time," said Mother.

Tallulah looked at her watch. "I think he is taking too much time."
"Much too much time," agreed Miranda.

"Time's up!" announced Adelaide.
Helmets on. Skates strapped and laced.
"To the park!"

Adelaide swung on the swings.

She slid down the slide.

She skated very fast.
"Yippee!"

Adelaide looked at Shelly.

"He is not ready," said Adelaide.
"Nope. Not ready like me at all."

"Maybe he is ready to be like me!" said Miranda.
She marched Shelly home and handed him a box
of crayons, a tray of paints, two brushes, a jar of
water, and a very large piece of paper.

She made paintings.
She made drawings.

"Voilà!"

Miranda looked at Shelly.

"He is not ready," said Miranda.
"Uh-uh. Not ready like me at all."

Tallulah stepped forward. "That's because he's
ready to be like me, me, me!" she sang out.

She kicked. She swirled.
And twirled, twirled, twirled.

"Ta-da!"

Tallulah looked at Shelly.

"He is definitely not you-know-what," she whispered
to Miranda and Adelaide.
"Not ready," they all agreed.

So Adelaide skated good-bye.

Miranda waved so long.

Tallulah ta-ta'd and skipped out the door.

It was quiet.
Shelly smiled.
He was ready for Shellytime.

He made a tent from sofa cushions. Safaris were exciting.

He chewed a big piece of pink gum and made a perfectly fine bubble.

He played Go Fish with his bunny, Edgar. The game ended in a tie.

He did a puzzle that had lots and lots of pieces.

He counted his toes. Five times.
That was a very big number.

He did one backward
somersault.

He read seven books,
built a house of blocks,

and made a sign for his door that said:
NO SISTERS ALLOWED.

Shelly had a very busy day.
A very fine Shelly busy day.

And then Adelaide, Miranda,
and Tallulah came home.

"Hmmf," said Adelaide with a *tsk, tsk, tsk.*
"Nope. Still not ready."

"Uh-uh," said Miranda with a woeful shake of her head. "Not ready."

"Definitely very not ready," said Tallulah with a perfect cartwheel.

Tallulah put her hands on her hips. "So? When, when, when will you be ready like me?"

"Or like me?" said Miranda.
"Or like me?" said Adelaide.

Shelly looked at his sisters.

He thought.
He grinned.

"Wednesday," he answered with a decided nod.

"Wednesday?" asked Adelaide.
"Wednesday?" asked Miranda.
"Wednesday?" asked Tallulah.

"Hooray! Yippee! Hoorah!" the three celebrated with a shout. They danced and jumped and circled the date on the calendar.

Shelly giggled. "Wednesday."

He just wasn't ready to
say which Wednesday.